The

Chosen One

Book 3 in the *"Stay in the Castle"* Series

By Pastor Jerry Ross

To order additional copies:

www.stayinthecastle.com

or call (812) 665-4375

Introduction

The name *Vala* means "chosen one." She was introduced in the last scene of *The Warrior Prince*, the second book of the *Stay in the Castle* series.

I needed to know her story. So, I decided to write it. Then, at some point, she began to tell it. That would make this a collaboration — of sorts.

I think you will have as much fun getting to know her as I did. Enjoy.

— Jerry Ross

That our daughters may be as corner stones,
polished after the similitude of a palace.
Psalms 144:12

Midnight Memories

The scream echoed off the inner walls of the castle.

Vala jerked awake, yanked from a sweet dream. The scream died then rose again more horrific than before. She threw back satin sheets and raced down the hall into their room. The two twins began to wail, huddled together on the bed they shared while Twain, their older brother, tried to shake Risa awake. His sister was staring but not seeing, then her face contorted and released another terror-drenched scream.

Vala pulled the boy gently away. "Light a candle, Twain."

She then slipped into Risa's bed, engulfed her from behind as another scream shook them both — little girl strawberry curls tangling with young woman raven-black, waist-length strands. Vala whispered prayers into her ear until the scream exhausted itself into a whimper. She then felt Risa stiffen, gathering air for another burst so Vala pressed hard against her, their heartbeats finding each other until Risa's began to slow, then some more, finally echoing that of Vala's. Risa's lungs slowly released the air they had gathered and her wide eyes fluttered, then closed, as her body surrendered and went limp. Vala's whispers continued for a time until the girl's soft, wet eyes opened, and looked around, herself again. "What happened?"

"You're screeching again, like a wild panther, scaring the twins to death!" Twain said, a bit too harshly, but more from relief than anger.

Vala's sweetness enveloped her. "You're safe."

****

Rinc, the warrior prince, was on sentry duty when he heard the scream. He walked his horse toward the east side of the castle, where the children were lodged — he did not hurry. This was not the first time he had heard the young girl's night terrors, although thankfully, they were becoming less frequent. He looked up at the high, dark window that suddenly blazed bright. He knew that Vala was now awake, caring for the situation. They would talk of it tomorrow, during their afternoon walk. He smiled in anticipation — it was the highlight of his day.

The "walk" was just one of his many assigned duties since he had arrived at the King's castle six months ago. The King had welcomed him then put him busy. Rinc was now in charge of the castle guards, as well as the training of the young princes, twelve years of age and older. He trained them hard, as his father had trained him — developing their physical strength, their endurance and agility. The King demanded each master the sword, so Rinc taught its skills, insisting on perfection, knowing a day would come when their lives would depend upon it.

The future warriors trained for battle in the morning, then after the mid-day meal, they were turned over to others who developed their given artisan skills. This freed Rinc to provide protection for the young ladies during their afternoon exercise, a walk led by Vala. The young princesses soon realized that the King had arranged this time so the young couple could get to know each other, so for part of the walk, they would skip ahead to allow the two to talk privately — as private as a couple can be with forty-two young giggling chaperones glancing constantly over their shoulders. He didn't mind. Her honor should be protected during their courtship, yet he did treasure the brief time they were "alone" each day.

Although he enjoyed this time in his life, his mind would often go back to the dark region of the kingdom where he had rescued the four orphans. The dragon had secured a strong-hold there, reducing the people to spiritual slaves. The King talked often of sending him there, of having him build a castle, battle the evil, promote good, and rescue whosoever would.

He wished to do all of these things. But first, he wished to win a young lady's heart. He wished for Vala.

****

The four children had arrived at the castle six months before, scared, starved, and sickly. They became Vala's personal charge from the day they arrived, and all were much the better for it. Their first meal, they ate themselves sick, fearful they might not be fed again, unable to believe they would be allowed to stay. The King had spent extra time with them during the first weeks, constantly assuring them that this was indeed their new home for as long as they wished. In the months since, a rosiness found its way into their pale faces and they added some weight to their skeletons. They then began their studies, slowly made new friends, and now had settled into the routine of castle life.

In small ways, they were still broken — Twain's fits of rage, still angry with himself, placing the blame of his mother's death on his ten-year-old shoulders; Risa's bubbly, happy personality shadowed at times by the dark memories of that nightmare village; the twins, though only four years old when rescued, still refusing to sleep without the other, plagued by a haunting insecurity. Broken, yes, but the King's love, the *Book of Lessons,* and Vala's care were now on their side.

Twain, still shaken by Risa's screams, came and sat beside Vala. "Is she always going to be like this?"

Risa snuggled close, and the two twins, Jozy and Gemma, — now hopelessly awake — leapt from their bed and ran to Vala, joining the midnight meeting.

"No, Risa will be fine. You all are going to be fine — no, better than fine, you're going to grow up and be extraordinary."

"I want to grow up and be like you," Risa sighed.

"You are going to grow up and be something better than me. You are going to be *you!* The one and only you. Someday you'll discover why the King rescued you, and his plan for you."

Jozy's head popped out from underneath the covers. "The King didn't rescue us, Prince Rinc did!"

7

Risa giggled. "Yes, silly. But it was the King who sent him. He was doing the King's bidding when he brought us here."

Vala smiled at the memory of their arrival — at the memory of *his* arrival. Four freshly orphaned urchins clinging to the back of a war horse led by a warrior prince — led by Rinc.

Risa, so wise for only eight years old, espied her smile and faraway stare. "You like him, don't you?"

Vala blushed, then changed the subject. "It's late, and you all need to get some sleep." The three youngest harmonized their protests. Instead of joining in, Twain sat quietly brooding.

"Tell me your thoughts, Twain."

He shifted uncomfortably, but then decided to speak. He could talk to Vala about things that he couldn't with anyone else. "How do you know we are going to be all right? I mean, things can happen — really bad things. And they seem to happen to, well, to children like us. We aren't from here — sometimes I feel we don't belong here — that we don't belong anywhere."

Vala reached over and took his hand. So much pain, so much damage done. "I know how you feel..."

Twain jerked his hand away. "No, you don't," he said with a sudden fierceness. "Don't say you do, because you don't. You have always had this — always been here — always been..." His eyes brimmed and he looked away.

Vala spoke with motherly authority. "Twain, look at me." Then, when he hesitated, "Please." He looked back, ashamed of his tears. "I have never lied to you, and I never will. I do not know all that you have been through, but the feelings you speak of, I do know them. This has not always been my home. Like you, I was brought here."

She now had the attention of all four. Gemma climbed onto her lap, then looked up in wonder. "You mean you haven't always been a princess?"

8

"No one now here was born here. We all were rescued — saved, if you will — by the King or someone he sent. What you four went through was horrible, but never think that others around you haven't suffered. And never indulge in self-pity. Never. Your past cannot rob you of a wonderful future unless you let it."

Risa stared at Vala as you might an unexpected surprise. "Vala, please tell us your story. We want…" she hesitated, overcome with emotion. "I *need* to know how you got here."

Vala wondered how the conversation had arrived where it had. She fought through a dozen different emotions, then quieted her heart. And listened. Eternity hinges on moments like these, and she didn't know what to do, what to share.

Then the guiding voice whispered, "It's time — tell it. Tell it all." So she did.

The Mountain Orphan

My strongest childhood memory is of the fire — of watching my home burn. The day my parents died.

Prior to that day, I had lived, in many ways, a very normal mountain-girl life. We scratched the earth, hunted and fished its meadows and streams, picked its herbs and berries, trapped its fur bearers, and gathered its firewood. All of this endless work barely kept the wolf from the door — we were dirt poor, but I was young and didn't know.

Sadly, I lived in a very abnormal mountain family. Poverty alone would not have mattered if it had been offset by love — but our home was bankrupt there also. My parents, as mid-teens, met too soon, mated too soon, married too soon, and realized it too late. They were two child-adults trying to raise a child. So they blamed each other for their poverty and misery and fought like panthers. Their fights often turned violent.

I was a reminder of their mistakes. Guilt, selfishness and immaturity makes for poor parenting, so I kept to myself and, for the most part was raising myself. I was less qualified than they were — so I grew wild, and willful, and increasingly wicked.

I was near the end of my eleventh year, the day I became an orphan. When my parents would fight — and they did a lot — I would sneak out my bedroom window, climb the hill, and dream of the day I could leave this place behind forever.

It was from that vantage point that I heard the gun shots, then watched our house explode in flames. I sat stunned. The black, billowing smoke eventually attracted the attention of some distant neighbors, and they arrived far too late to do any-thing but watch the inferno. Charred walls weakened under the blazing roof until everything crashed down upon itself. In just a few hours, everything I knew — my parents, my home, my life — all reduced to smoke, soot and ashes.

I wandered down to stand beside the small group of spectators, until someone finally noticed me. A woman knelt down and began to question me, but my mind was whirling, and I felt wooden — not myself — then the world spun away as I col-lapsed into the dirt.

****

Hours later, I woke in a dark room, dark except for the moonlight fighting its way through a small pane of mud-streaked glass. The room was small, but I was not alone. Other children lounged around the room, all watching me, all quietly staring.

I could hear a man and woman arguing, shouting at each other, in the next room. I shut my eyes, listened hard, and soon realized the fight was about me.

The woman wanted to take me in, but her man was hav-ing none of it. "Already have too many mouths to feed," "Don't need someone else's troubles," "Not our business" — on and on he went. I heard a knock on the cabin's door, then another voice, a man's, but quieter. I could not discern his words, but soon I heard the door close as he left. Then a thin shaft of light cut into the room, slicing me in two.

"She awake?" I kept my eyes closed as the other children stared back at the man peeking into the room. "Doesn't matter. Seems like her mother has a sister. She should be here some time tomorrow to fetch her." With that, he closed the door and recommenced arguing with the woman.

Questions whirled in my head. "My mother has a sister?" "I have an aunt?" "Tomorrow she's coming to get me?"

I lay still, faking sleep. Tears rivered my cheeks as I thought back over the day. How could they leave me? Gunfire, house fire, and my life caught in the cross-fire — gone. Just like that. Did they even think of me as they destroyed each other?

****

I sat most of the day on the front step, my hands folded in my lap, wearing the only dress I owned, staring at my bare feet and waiting. Lunch time came and went, but I was not invited to the table. Finally, the woman walked out and tossed the heel of a small loaf of bread into my lap. She started to speak, but her husband yelled something and she whirled away.

I dozed the afternoon away, leaning against the porch post, then woke to the noise of a racing wagon. The driver lashing the twin horses was a fierce-looking woman, untamed red hair blowing, her eyes piercing me as she skidded to a stop.

"You Mara's kid?" she demanded. I stared, frozen in fear, finally managing a slight nod. "Then get in, I don't have all day."

The man and woman came onto the porch. She reached down and pushed me gently toward the wagon. As I climbed in, the man gauged its value and the two horses pulling it.

"We cared for your niece like she was our own," he lied. "Fed her, lodged her… we rescued her from the fire — we'd be right to expect to be paid for our troubles."

My aunt stared at him, disgusted. "It's not like you did me any favors. Now I'm saddled with a kid I don't want. Whatever you did was your neighborly duty, so don't expect a hand-out for it." With that, she whipped the team and they jumped in the traces, and away we sped down the mountain.

That was my introduction to Thira the Red.

****

Twain touched her arm. "I'm sorry. I didn't know."

"Of course you didn't. But I need you to know what happened, so that you can know you'll be all right."

"I appreciate it, but you don't have to relive it."

Risa faced her brother. "Yes she does!" Then to Vala, "You have to finish the story!"

Vala laughed. "Wouldn't be fair to quit now. Besides, it is part of what has made me who I am today."

Risa noticed the twins, both now asleep. "How can they sleep through this?"

"It's God's gift to the young. It is best they sleep. I'm going to share with you some grown-up things. You are blessed to be here — to have arrived now, at your ages. When things change — when both of you change — never be tempted to return to the world. Don't go back into the dark."

Vala looked back into her darkness, hugged herself for courage, then continued.

Turpis Villa

Thira raced through the night — the dark seemed her light, as she slowed not at all. At some point, exhaustion overtook me, and I remember no more of the trip. She shook me awake as we drove through the gate of her estate, the sun now fully risen on a place called Turpis Villa.

All I had known was our mountain shack, so I stared in disbelief. Turpis Villa squatted on two acres of ground at the edge of a large, active village. The property was encased on three sides by seven foot, wrought iron fencing. The house was a three-story, oak beamed and river stoned construction. The bottom floor housed a tavern and eatery, the second, rooms for rent, and the third, the office and living quarters of Thira the Red. Several women lounged on the front porch as two servants scurried to meet the wagon and care for the hard-driven horses.

I scarcely had time to take it in as Thira barked orders at me as soon as we stopped. There was no warmth to the woman. She didn't want me, and told me so from that first day.

"I told your mother she was a fool marrying that drifter. Dirt marrying dirt. And look what they hatched out." Then for no reason, she slapped me so hard my ears rang. "You'll earn your keep and then some, I promise you that."

One of the women cackled at my tears. "My, my, Red — where did you get that pretty little thing? So she's your niece?"

"She's whatever I say she is! Watch your tongue, and go fetch Atgas for me. Tell her to get the girl settled and then put her to work." Thira tornadoed away, satin skirts sashaying, barking more orders, leaving me in the dust of her disappearance.

That day I turned twelve and no one even noticed.

****

I was handed over to Atgas, a cruel, evil woman who oversaw the care of the manor. She was in charge of the household slaves, the cooks, and the cleaning girls — me, and as I was later to find out, two other girls, one older and one a mite younger. Atgas carried a leather crop, crafted for use on livestock or horses, but her purpose was not to drive animals, but servant girls who slowed or slacked.

13

"Where are your things?"

I looked at the ground, embarrassed. "Everything was lost in the fire…"

"Speak up, child!" she screeched at me.

I was scared to speak, and she grabbed my arm and dragged me toward the back of the property to a small shed. Its heavy door stood open, and I could not help but notice the massive padlock that hung on its hasp. Inside, were three pallets, a battered wardrobe, and a table and one chair. There was a pitcher for water, a basin for washing, and a chamber pot on the floor beside. It smelled like an outhouse. The shed was unpainted and ungarnished yet solidly constructed, and I was shocked to see bars on the windows. It was more a prison than a home.

Atgas pointed, "This is where you will sleep. Since you failed to bring a change of clothes, I'll find another dress for you. You will work and do as you're told or you'll wish you had. Now, come along — it's time to start earning your keep!"

A few minutes later, I was on my hands and knees, scrub brush in hand, with a bucket of hot lye water alongside. Atgas stood over me that day, shouting and cursing me as I scoured every inch of the kitchen floor. My tears mingled with the soapy water beneath me, but I worked as I never had, fearful of the lash of her crop. I couldn't believe this was now my life.

****

An hour before dark, I was herded into the kitchen, to a small corner table, where two other girls sat and stared. I greeted them and received a knot from Atgas's crop on the back of my head as a reward.

"No talking!"

I sat with my head bowed, avoiding eye contact and, hopefully, another bruise. Every muscle in my body ached, and I was famished. The cook brought a large portion of thick stew and the heel end of a loaf, and the three of us ate in silence. The food was delicious, and for that I was thankful.

All three of us were then marched to the shed, the door slammed and padlocked behind us. I dared not speak till Atgas disappeared back into the main house, then I turned rubbing my head, getting my first good look at the other two girls.

"My name is Vala. Who are you?"

The youngest spoke first. "You mustn't anger Atgas. Don't ever speak to us outside this room, and even in here only when no one is near." Though she was only nine years old, there was an edge to her, a fire that burned just under the surface. This place had bent her, but had failed to break her. I instantly liked her.

I rubbed the knot on my head. "Thanks, but I already figured that out. What's your name?"

"I'm Adeen. Her name is Pembroke, but she answers to Pem. She doesn't talk — never has that I know of." Pem walked over to me, reached out past my extended hand and touched my hair. She looked to be a few years older than me, wide mouth, high cheekbones, with blond, shoulder length hair. Pem was on the verge of blossoming into womanhood, yet her blue eyes still shone with a childlike innocence. She smiled at me, but her eyes held a great sadness, the likes I had never seen. She touched my cheek, then turned away and went to her pallet on the floor, laid down with her back to us, and pulled the small blanket over her.

"I've only been here three months. Pem? Not sure how long, but I think most of her life. She's a hard worker, and most here like her — except Thira and Atgas — they hate everyone."

The dim light of the dying day shadowed Adeen's features. She was in many ways a miniature version of Thira — same wild red hair, but a stronger, honest, though thickly freckled face. She told me she was recently orphaned, her mother had contracted a fever, then died four days later. She didn't

15

have a father, and her only surviving relative was her grand-mother who succumbed to the same sickness a week later. The village elders didn't know what to do with her, so they had brought her to Turpis Villa and asked if Thira the Red could use her as a servant girl. A free slave was enticing, but Thira first refused, until the elders included a bag of silver coins and a milk cow. Anything to rid them of this unwanted girl.

"So what's your story?"

I told her of my mountain life, my parents, the fire, and the appearance of an aunt that I didn't know existed.

"Mercy! If you are her niece, you'd think she'd treat you better, but nothing surprises me with that woman. Cruelty curdles her brain! The only thing that makes her smile is more silver in her pockets — she's probably mad at you because you didn't come with a milk cow and coins."

I laughed. No, I was no bargain. But my aunt seemed determined to make up for it by working my fingers to the bone.

"Why the padlock and barred windows?"

"You, me and Pem are just three more things Thira owns. Keeps us from running away. But trust me, there are times that you will be glad for the locked door and bars."

"Glad? Why?"

"What do you think this place is? A boarding house? Your aunt is not a good person. She makes money off of watered down rum, good food and sinful men. Sometimes, one of her drunken guests will sneak back and try to get in to us. Vala, what feels like a prison can sometimes actually be protection."

She yawned a big yawn. "We best get some sleep. Tomorrow isn't going to be any easier."

I lay awake awhile, listening to their breathing, thinking of Pem's sadness, wondering what she would tell me if she could. And of Adeen's words. I had often viewed my mountain shack and simple ways a prison. A single tear escaped my eye, then exhaustion took hold. I dreamed that night of home.

****

Rinc rode the perimeter of the castle grounds. A few clouds shrouded the moon off and on, as it waxed valiantly towards fullness. Each time he passed east of the castle, he saw that the candle light still burned in the children's room. It had been an hour since the screams. Maybe Risa needed the light for comfort — or the twins, afraid of the dark. More than likely, Vala still sat with them, telling them stories or singing softly.

He first fell in love with her voice — that first meeting, when she had curtsied and called him brave. He had stood there unable to utter a word; the memory brought a grin as he remembered her playful smile. He wondered, had she felt the same?

They talked of many things on their afternoon walks, but much of her past remained shrouded. As he chatted on about his parents and castle upbringing, he sensed in her a sadness. The King had hinted that she had not enjoyed a sheltered childhood — that Rinc should be patient. She would tell him all her heart when she trusted his heart. He purposed to earn her trust.

There were also things he had not shared. He told Vala the story of finding the four orphans and of the dark village. They wondered how many other families needed rescued — the region needed a lord, a castle, to bring hope. Rinc had told her of finding Angus, but had not shared with her the story of Parisa. One day he must and wondered what her reaction would be.

He froze, his warrior senses on high alert. The forest began a mile from the west side of the castle, and from its edge he saw a small glimmer, ever slight, a reflection of moonlight on metal. He held his horse perfectly still, eyes narrow, focusing. For the next hour, he watched. The glimmer did not repeat itself, but his warrior training never doubted what it saw.

Someone was out there.

Sister Survivors

Risa's eyes widened, totally lost in the story. "They locked you in a shed? What happened to Adeen and Pem? Did you get away?"

Twain laughed, "No, donkey, she's still in there."

Risa stuck out her tongue at him. Vala laughed at their brother-sister antics. They would poke at each other, but Vala knew beneath the surface, they were fiercely loyal. Tragedy and trial had forged an ironclad bond between them.

"Yes, I did get out. By God's grace, I was eventually rescued from my nightmare. But at a great sacrifice — a sacrifice I did not deserve and will never be able to repay..."

The mood of the room changed — the two twins slept on, a brother and sister stared in silence, and a castle princess wiped tears and then went back into her nightmare.

****

A year passed. I grew five inches and turned thirteen. My feet seemed too big, the rest of me, all knees and elbows, as I entered that gangly, girlish, awkward time of growing. My body had hardened to the work, and I could measure my strength against the time I had first arrived. Labor became less difficult, but the days no shorter.

A close, sweet friendship grew between me, Adeen and Pem. We talked of what we would be, what we would do when we eventually escaped this place. Well, Adeen and I talked — Pem just smiled and listened.

Pem had blossomed into a true beauty. Her smile brightened our evenings, as we sat and listened to Adeen's endless chatter. Adeen could weave amazing stories of imaginary places, too wonderful to be real. Her favorite, of a King who adopted orphans, taking them to his castle and rearing them as his own. She swore it was true, that her mother had told her of this place.

Suddenly, she stopped and looked at me, so serious, so sure.

"Vala, one day, you are going to be a princess." I laughed, thinking she jested. She just stared, like she was seeing me for the first time. "It's true. I can't explain it, but some things I just... see. You'll be a princess, and your life is going to be spent making a difference — helping people, saving people."

"And what about you, Adeen? What do you see for your life?" I asked smiling, still thinking this one of her games.

"My purpose? My life?" She stared past me, then smiled such a sad smile. "To see that you get that chance." And with that, she stood, walked to her pallet, and lay down. I looked at Pem and she opened her mouth, as if to speak — wanting to tell me something, warn me of something. She finally just smiled her sad, secret smile. And with that, we too laid down to sleep.

****

In the months that followed, we fell into a routine as we survived the long, laborious days and locked-up nights. The seasons turned, and soon I was nearing my fourteenth birthday. Some days were bad, and others, not-so-bad. Atgas would hardly speak to us for days, choosing instead to gossip with the front-porch women or flirt with the stable hands. Then she would pick a day, determined to bully one of us mercilessly. Her cruelty at times was boundless.

On one such day, it was Adeen's turn, and as hard as she tried, she could do nothing right in Atgas's eyes. I hated to see her mistreated, and longed for the day I would be old enough and strong enough to fight back.

Atgas followed Adeen to the creek, screaming every step of the way. Adeen struggled back with a full bucket, never fast enough for her tormentor, water sloshing as she came. Almost to the porch, she tripped and fell, splashing water on Atgas's legs and feet. A rage took hold of her like I had never seen. She stood over Adeen and began to beat her with the crop, savagely striking her body and head. The devil was in her, and I knew she wouldn't stop till she killed her.

I ran from the back porch and threw myself over my small friend, gathering her under me. Atgas kicked and cursed me. "You want her beating? Fine with me!" And with that, she unleashed on me — the leather crop stinging my back, again and again. I gritted my teeth, determined not to cry out. Atgas was completely mad, and I remember thinking that I would die here.

Suddenly, the whip stopped, and Atgas cried out. I glanced up to see Thira pulling her backwards by her hair, then throwing her hard to the ground.

"You trying to kill them? Well, get up and go ahead! But you'll do all their work instead." Atgas lay there shaking, the wild anger still in her, but afraid to speak back to her boss.

I looked under me at Adeen, who was wide-eyed and frightened, then glanced back to my aunt in time to see her unleash a kick into my side that lifted me off Adeen, and landed me on my back, hard on the ground. The air went out of me, and I struggled to breathe. She leaned over me and spat.

"I probably should have let her kill you both. All you do is cost me money and cause aggravation. But your day will come — another year and I'll get my money back and more."

She then turned to Atgas. "Lock them in the shed. Don't feed them the rest of the day. And bring me Pem when she's done with her chores. I'll need her this evening."

Atgas picked up herself, then her crop, and I was sure she would start beating us again, but her insanity had passed, although her hatred still burned. I avoided looking at her.

"Get up and get moving," she said in a dangerous, even tone. I helped Adeen up, and we made our way to the shed. I placed myself between the two, and gently guided Adeen through the door. As we entered, Atgas gave me a vicious kick in the middle of my back, sending us both sprawling on the ground.

"I'd kill you if it wasn't for the money you'll bring. Your time will come, and I'll be the one laughing then." She slammed the door and snapped the padlock, then stormed away.

We spent some time nursing our wounds, but we were more worried about Pem than ourselves. Thira had never cared a whit about Pem. What did she want with her? Pem always spent her evenings with us, locked away. What had changed?

Darkness fell as the sun dipped behind the western hills. There was more activity than usual around the manor. We gazed out the barred window, a sense of unexplained dread upon us.

Adeen was unusually quiet. I finally went to her, and she buried her face in my chest and wept. She was so tough that it was easy to forget that she was still just a little girl. She looked up at me, fear spilling from her eyes. "Pem should be here — with us." I held her tighter, not sure what to say.

Music started in the house, and guests started to arrive. It did not seem the usual crowd, more carriages than usual, more wealth than normal. Then, up the lane came an exquisite black carriage, pulled by four midnight-black horses. Two outriders flanked the carriage, each on matching black stallions, each heavily armed. The carriage stopped near the front door, and Thira the Red floated out to greet her guest, dolled up in a flowing gown, piled hair and green, feathered hat. She cooed her greetings, the door of the carriage opened, and Evil stepped out.

****

Rinc walked his horse slowly toward the castle gate, whispering to the guards, placing them on alert. He explained to them what he saw, and though he did not think the danger imminent, he was not going to take any chances.

The best course of action was to wait for first light, then lead a small brigade on a quick ride directly to the forest's edge. Something or someone was out there, spying on the castle. He needed to know who and why.

His months here at the castle had dulled the razor-edge vigilance he had when traveling the King's Highway. He rebuked himself for it. What had his mother said? "The dragon — you cannot let down your guard or underestimate his cunning..."

It had been a week since he had last scouted that portion of the forest. Too long. It was so easy to get comfortable — to forget diligence. Again, he chided himself, then refocused, going over his plan of action. Tomorrow he would get his answers.

****

Ubel, the Dark Lord

Thira eyed the devil that stepped out of that dark carriage. His name was Ubel and they were partners of sort. He was a rich and powerful lord, whose holdings stretched from here westward, to the dark region of the kingdom. Ubel lived in a stone fortress, and his income came from extortion, robbery, gambling, weak beer, strong rum, and the slave trade.

Once a year, he would spend several months making his rounds, visiting his financial interests — thirty or so places like Thira's. Ubel supplied Thira with the booze she sold, protection against her enemies, and the building and property where she conducted her business. In return, he received the lion's share of her profits. Ubel always carried with him gold aplenty, and the dark lord was rich enough to buy whatever suited his eye. He was ruthless, ruling his financial kingdom with an iron fist.

Down deep, Thira and Ubel hated each other, distrusted each other, and tried to take advantage of each other. Yet they needed each other to grow rich. She dreaded his yearly visits and resented the money he'd take. This time, Thira intended to keep as much of her gold and silver as possible.

"Ubel, my lord," she cooed as he approached. "I have a grand party arranged in your honor."

He smiled an evil smile, well aware of her wiles. "And a

party we will enjoy, Thira. But then we will do business. I have to leave here in the..." his sentenced left unfinished as he spied the young lady on the porch. "Thira, who have we here?"

Thira feigned surprise, as she looked behind her. "Oh, just one of my servant girls. I needed an extra hand serving the food tonight — it's hard to make ends meet with the constant increase in overhead." Thira then motioned her forward. "Come, child. I want you to meet our most honored guest."

From the shadows, a young lady stepped toward them, dressed in splendor, shadowed in sadness.

****

Adeen cried out in horror. "Thira is going to sell her! She's going to sell Pem to that evil man!" During the past two years, we had seen Ubel come and go a few times, but thought little of it since it did not affect our existence. Until now.

I looked out through the window bars unable to grasp what I saw. I hardly recognized Pem — the porch women must have spent hours getting her ready for this moment. Pem looked like a princess — trussed up in finery, satin shoes, hair meticulously styled, rouge generously applied — she was breathtaking.

"Even my aunt is not that evil." The minute I said it, I did not believe it. Yes, Thira the Red would do anything for another ounce of gold or bag of silver. I felt physically ill.

Adeen held my hand as I fought to breathe. "Vala, pull yourself together. We have to do something!" I sat on the floor, my back against the wall, my head spinning. The wooden wall cut into the fresh, bloody stripes on my back. I looked through tears at Adeen's bruised face and blood-streaked hair. We were bolted in, beaten, broken, and helpless to stop the evil that controlled our lives.

"Vala!" Adeen cried, desperate for me to do something.

"Adeen, tell me what to do! If I could give my life for

Pem, I would right now! We can't get out and if we could there is Thira and Atgas and armed guards. Tell me, and I'll do it!"

Utter despair — that is all we had left and I hated how it felt. Adeen came into my arms and we wept together, two broken, helpless girls trapped in a nightmare of fear.

And from the back porch, we could hear Atgas laughing.

****

Risa and Twain were both in tears. If there was something they could relate to, it was helplessness.

"He took her, didn't he?"

"Yes, Twain. Adeen and I slept not a wink that night, both holding each other, staring out the window, weeping as the music played. Just after midnight, Ubel's two guards brought Pem out of the house and put her into the carriage. A few minutes later, Thira came out, escorted by Ubel, chatting and laughing like old friends. Money exchanged hands, he bowed, she curtsied, and then he stepped into the carriage. We strained to see into the darkness of the carriage, but its shadows swallowed our friend. We never saw her again."

Vala could see the anger building in Twain and felt Risa sink into despair. She knew they were reliving their own nightmare, their own desperate helplessness to stop the evil that had destroyed their parents.

"So evil wins again," he whispered bitterly.

"Yes, sometimes it does. Or seems to for now. But that is why we must prepare. We cannot undo the evils of the past, but we can fight against the evils not yet committed. We can overcome evil with good."

Twain wanted to believe what Vala said, but was struggling mightily with memories and emotions. "What can *we* do?"

Vala turned and looked fully into both children's eyes.

"We take the fight to them. The King wants Rinc to build a castle right in the middle of Ubel's stronghold. This will take time, and the battle will be long, but the King promises us his power and presence. There are still girls like Pem waiting to be rescued and good people like your parents, who need the strong sword of a warrior prince. Twain, we will need warriors. So you have to decide — you can spend your life the bitter victim of evil, or with the King's help, you can spend your life as a victor of good."

Risa, ever listening, never missing a thing, smiled. "You said *we* — 'we will need warriors'."

Vala blushed again. "Yes, I did. Can I share something with the two of you, something you will keep in your hearts?" They nodded, all ears. "I do not want to seem presumptuous. But, my guiding voice — do you know what I mean by that?"

Risa nodded immediately. Twain, thought for a moment, then spoke. "I think so. I was afraid to speak of it, afraid I would be thought crazy."

Vala smiled. "My guiding voice spoke to me the day I met Rinc. I believe he is the one prepared for me, and I for him. There is a familiarity, a calm knowing, when we are together. I don't know how to explain it, but I pray that God will grow and bless it. Yes, I said *we*. And if the King wills, and Rinc asks, I would be honored to be his wife. I would embrace the chance to do all I could to help him establish a stronghold for good. I owe that to Pem. And I especially owe it to Adeen."

Both children sat still, three souls now one. They waited, not asking for her to finish the story. Both knew she would — both knew she needed to. That she must.

No Greater Love

Every day we missed our friend, and every night we prayed for her. Life fell back into its miserable routine. In the days after Pem's departure, Atgas watched us with hawk eyes, never far away, expecting us to exact some revenge or attempt an escape. Adeen and I had secretly agreed to appear docile and broken, but we were ever watchful, determined to find a way to escape our nightmare. At night we would discuss dozens of plans, none of which had a chance of working.

Another year slipped by. We marked the days, dreading Ubel's return while also wishing for it, with some hope that he would bring Pem with him. That year was the year of my blossoming. Adeen said it was like watching a caterpillar turn into a butterfly — but she said so in fear. I noticed the stable hands staring more, and would sometimes hear the porch women make crude comments, but what I hated most was the measured looks I would get from Thira. It was as if she were gauging the weight of a prize hog to determine if it was ready to slaughter.

I spoke of my fear to Adeen, telling her that I would kill myself rather than be taken away by Ubel. She told me to have faith. "Vala, I have seen you in my dreams — you will be a princess. There is a great life ahead for you, trust me."

This wild, red-haired, freckled twelve-year-old looked so confident — had such great faith — and I loved her for it.

****

A week later, we woke and prepared for another day, but Atgas failed to show up to unlock the door. We watched out the window, noticed the extra activity, and feared what we knew it meant. Ubel was coming.

An hour before dark, Atgas came. As she was unlocking the door, Adeen whispered my way, "Remember, trust me." Then she lay down on her pallet and feigned sleep.

Atgas opened the door, and looked warily around, took note of Adeen sleeping, then turned her attention toward me. Her smile was pure evil. I sat in our only chair, petrified.

"Get up! You're a lucky girl! You get to attend a party

26

tonight." She threw back her head and laughed, and when she did Adeen sprang upon her with such fury that it took me by surprise. She leapt on her back, scratching at her eyes and face, with tiger determination. Atgas whirled around then crashed backwards into the wall violently crushing Adeen, causing her to lose her grip, slide down to her waist, then on to the ground. Adeen curled into a ball, as Atgas kicked her and struck her with her crop. I stood and screamed her name, "Atgas!"

She whirled my way, expecting an attack, but instead I stood still. "I'll go. I'm ready. Just, please — stop hurting her."

She looked down at Adeen, kicked her once more, then said, "Fine. I'll have plenty of time to deal with her later." She shook the crop my way. "Let's go, and no trouble!"

And I did. Atgas stopped long enough to snap the padlock shut, then poked the crop into my back. I took a step, then another, surrendering to my fate.

****

Adeen stayed huddled on the floor and counted to fifty — making sure that Atgas was gone. Then she crept to the window and watched Vala and Atgas enter the back door of the house.

Then she smiled.

Adeen opened her clenched fist and stared at the faded red cord tied around the key to the door's padlock — the key she had just taken from Atgas's pocket during the attack. Then she prayed a quick prayer and waited for the sun to finish setting.

****

I was turned over to four of the porch women who ushered me into a private room where they had a bath drawn and new clothes laid out. They made a big fuss over me, laughing, joking, and telling me how beautiful I was. I was sleep walking in the middle of a nightmare, with no hope of waking up.

****

Adeen had replayed every detail of the night they took Pem — replayed it in her mind a thousand times. Her hope — her only hope — was that tonight would follow a similar pattern. She wanted to tell Vala her plan, but Vala had no guile. Her soul was too pure. She would give it away with a look in the wrong direction at the wrong time. No, it had to be this way.

An hour after dark, Ubel's black carriage arrived — same driver and same two armed horsemen flanking the rear. They dismounted, looped their reins onto the back of the carriage, and stood at attention, as Thira came out — different dress but same false flattery. She watched Ubel stare into the porch — just like the night Pem was taken. Adeen closed her eyes tightly, fighting the tears. Vala stepped out, breathtakingly beautiful.

Adeen began to panic, self-doubt cascading over her. What if this doesn't work? She couldn't lose Vala also. She slowed her breath and quieted her heart. And prayed.

She dragged the chair to the door, and stood on it, reaching out between the window bars to the padlock below. She had practiced this at night several times as Vala slept, and knew she could reach it. She felt for the lock and slipped in the key. It turned easily and clicked open. She then slid it carefully off the hasp and lifted both the key and the padlock back to her.

The night they took Pem, the party had lasted till the moon was straight above — about four hours she thought. The driver and two horsemen had hung around the carriage for the first hour or so, then began to flirt with some of the porch women. Food and drinks had been offered and accepted — leaving the carriage for a short time unattended. Then the guards had been called in to accompany Pem to the carriage, and the driver had taken his place, as Ubel said his lengthy goodbyes. Money then had been exchanged before they rode away.

Adeen cracked open the door, tied a bundle to her back, and slipped out of the shed. She began to make a wide loop, gradually making her way to the far side of the carriage. Halfway there, she reached into the firewood pile and pulled out a three-foot, stout piece of oak. Adeen flexed the muscles of her arms, glad now for what hard labor had created. She would only have one chance. "God, please, give me strength."

****

My trance was interrupted as Ubel's two henchmen each took an arm and guided me up, out of my chair. My mind had ceased to function at some time during the evening, and the party sounds seemed to come from miles away. I knew I was walking, and the night air told me that I was outside. The driver climbed to his seat, as the door of the enclosed carriage was opened and I was firmly lifted and placed inside. Ubel was saying his goodbyes. I saw Thira receive a small bag, and vaguely wondered what my life — my future — was worth. The armed guards stood at attention, waiting for their master. I noticed Atgas, in the shadows behind Thira, smirking into the carriage, taunting. I searched her eyes but found no soul.

****

Atgas had hated Pem. She hated Vala. She was a bitter woman, ugly in heart and soul. Her hatred was not personal — Atgas just hated anything beautiful or good.

This was her triumph. Ubel would destroy anything of worth in Vala. Pretty soon, she would be as broken and ugly inside as Atgas. That was her revenge.

She stared hard into Vala's eyes, determined to enjoy every second of her misery. But then, something lifted out of the luggage hold on top the carriage, behind the driver — some nightmarish demon, or God-sent angel. Its hair flamed in the reflection of the porch lights as it raised a rod of judgment. Atgas opened her mouth to shout a warning, but the imp's warrior cry froze her in place, rending the night, as she swung the club at the head of the driver.

****

Adeen waited till the driver was seated, felt the carriage rock as Vala was loaded, then waited ten seconds more. She needed every eye on Ubel. As she slowly rose, she thought of Pem, of Vala, of all the beatings — and channeled this into the violence of her swing. The wild cry was unplanned. It just erupted out of her and probably saved them. It froze everyone for the precious few seconds she needed. As the body of the driver hit the ground, Adeen jumped into his place, grabbed the reins, released the brake and lashed the horses. The animals, already on edge because of the unnatural scream, jerked the carriage into instant motion. Armed guards raced to their mounts, only to watch them stampede ahead still tied to the carriage.

The scene Adeen left behind was pandemonium. Thira screamed, and men were running in all directions. The last voice Adeen heard was Ubel's, as he roared for Thira to bring him a horse. Both of the war horses broke free of the carriage a half-mile down the road, and ran along side for another quarter-mile.

Adeen raced down the mountain road, desperate to put distance between her and Turpis Villa — determined that neither she nor Vala would ever return. She had bought them some time, and only that. After five more miles at a cannonball pace, she pulled hard on the reins, slowing the horses until they stopped in a cloud of dust.

****

I had no idea what was happening.

First a wild scream, then the carriage driver fell, landing with a thud. I looked out and saw everyone — Ubel, Thira, Atgas, the servants and porch women — all staring in disbelief at the top of the carriage. It shook as someone landed in the driver's seat, then I was jerked out of my seat onto the floor of the carriage, as we shot forward.

The next several minutes were terrifying. I managed to pull myself up off the floor and onto the seat, then held on for dear life. Dark trees raced by the windows. Who was driving?

Whoever he was, he seemed heaven-sworn to kill us both.

Finally, mercifully, the carriage slowed, then stopped. I heard someone set the brake, then skirts and red hair jumped down and yanked open the carriage door. Adeen seemed a vision — a sunbeam of hope bursting into my darkest nightmare. She reached in and pulled me out.

"You saved us. We got away!" I screamed hysterically.

Adeen pulled me down onto my knees so that she could look me in the eye. "Vala, you need to listen and do exactly what I say. Are you listening?"

I nodded, trying to grasp the reality of her standing there.

"Ubel and his men will be coming. They will eventually catch up to the carriage. I have a plan, but you have to do what I tell you." Adeen shoved a cloth bundle into my arms. "I packed you a change of clothes and leather shoes. Change as soon as you can and get rid of that dress. Bury it or hide it somewhere. There is also some food that I pilfered."

"But aren't you coming with me?"

Adeen smiled her self-assured smile. "No, I have to lead them on for a ways. If we both leave the road here, they will find the carriage and then track us down in no time."

I started to protest, but Adeen put her hand over my mouth. "Vala, I've got it all figured out. Don't worry, we'll always be together." She pulled my face to hers. "Vala — I got us this far, didn't I? Now please, trust me and do as I say."

I was still in shock at the turn of events. I nodded numbly, then stood to my feet. Adeen climbed up into the driver's seat and started to release the brake, then stopped. She looked down, broad smile and all, wild hair and all. "You should have seen Thira's face." She laughed out loud, and for the first time that day, I smiled. "Now go into the forest and hide until Ubel and his men ride by. Then make your way to freedom — freedom, Vala. Travel by night and stay hidden during the day."

"But I thought..."

Adeen interrupted me, her eyes now wet. "Vala, you are going to be a princess. You will see that I was right. And when it happens, I need you to do one thing for me. Just one."

Tears coursed my cheeks as I looked up at my wild little survivor sister. "Anything."

"One of these days, after you are safe and when you grow strong — you go find Pem. Find her, Vala. Free her and give her a good life. She deserves it. Now promise."

My answer came out as a whisper. "I promise."

Adeen smiled one more unforgettable smile, started to speak, then couldn't find the words. So she winked instead, released the brake, and whipped the horses into action. I stood in the road, staring after her until she rounded the bend, disappearing in a tornado of dust. I had sleep-walked out of a nightmare, still not believing this was real.

The sound of hoofbeats, thundering in the distance, broke my trance and sent me scurrying into the forest. A few minutes later, three riders sped by, whipping their horses down the road. It finally hit me what Adeen was doing. I looked up the mountain slope, suddenly frantic for my friend. I clawed my way upward, determined to find a vantage point so I could see the road below. As I climbed, I began to sob, calling out for Adeen.

****

The road became a series of mountain switchbacks, slowing drastically the pace of the carriage. Still, Adeen drove the horses as furiously as she dared. She glanced back over her shoulder and saw Ubel's horse bearing down from behind, two other riders following in hot pursuit. The road straightened, and she whipped the horses forward, but they were no match for the speed of Ubel's war horse. He rode alongside the carriage, cursing at her to stop. She smiled at him and drove the horses on.

Ubel roared in anger, then leapt from his horse onto the back of the carriage. He almost fell, secured a hold then slowly climbed up to where the redheaded girl sat. She glanced behind, saw him creeping toward her, then did the strangest thing.

She laughed. Loud and long.

He looked ahead at a sharp curve in the road, then realized they would never make the turn. He stood and hurled himself from the carriage just as Adeen drove the horses off the mountain into a rocky gorge. He landed hard on the mountain face, then bounced, bones breaking, then ricocheted into the rocks below. As he landed, he heard a loud crash, and the scream of the horses as the carriage, rider, and passenger all smashed themselves onto the gorge's rocky floor. What he did not hear — what no one heard — was the terrible scream a mile above, from a young beauty who watched it all in the moonlight.

****

The two children now held the princess as she wept. They were glad to be there for her as she had so often been for them.

After a while she grew quiet, then spoke. "I wandered for a week, afraid to go into any village, afraid someone would take me back to Turpis Villla. I soon ran out of food, and stumbled half starved onto a mountain farm, not so unlike the one of my childhood. The husband and wife who owned the farm had never been able to have children of their own, and they took me in and cared for me till I was able to regain my strength.

I finally told them my story, and they took pity, assuring me that they would keep me safe. The farmer made a trip into town to hear the available gossip and came back with fearful news. The story of Ubel, the carriage crash, and a missing girl was the talk of the town. Ubel had been pulled from the rocks by his two soldiers, and nearly died from his injuries. How seriously he was hurt no one knew, but it was rumored that his one arm was so mangled, amputation was necessary.

A few days later, men were sent to recover the bodies of the beautiful young woman and the crazed runaway girl driving the carriage. Only one body was found.

Ubel immediately posted a reward — a helmet filled with gold — for anyone who could locate me. I feared the farmer and his wife would give into greed and take me to Ubel. The farmer's wife dispelled my fears.

'We know Ubel. His wickedness is a blight upon this whole region. Rest easy. We will see to it you receive safe passage to a safe place.'

A week later, I was smuggled in a wagon filled with fresh hay, into the castle of a kind lord, who lived by the *Book of Lessons*, and told me of his King — one who adopted orphans and made them royalty. It seems Adeen's mother was right."

****

Risa and Twain went willingly to their beds, exhausted. They would look back forever on this night, and they would never be the same because of it. Neither would Vala.

She dressed, then went to find the King. He was up on the ramparts, looking out toward the west. He smiled as she came and curtsied. "How was your night, Vala?"

How to answer? "Long, but well spent." She paused, then pressed on. "Your highness, I have a request — I need to talk to Rinc. There are some things... it will take some time and require a measure of privacy." She blushed, not wanting to be misunderstood. She need not fear. The King always understood.

"I agree." He smiled knowingly. "Later this morning, you two will be given as much time as you need. For now, our warrior prince is doing his duty." She followed his eyes as Rinc and a troop of castle guards rode, encircling the distant forest.

****

He rode back an hour later. The King and Vala met him at the front gate. "Someone has been watching the castle from the forest. It appears they have been doing so for several days."

A chill ran down Vala's spine. The King looked her way, concerned. "Prince Rinc, I need you to free up the rest of your morning. Place the castle guards on alert, then escort Vala to the castle courtyard. There are some things the two of you need to talk about."

Rinc glanced at her, and she at him. Never had she looked so serious, so vulnerable. He issued orders, then walked with her, and for the next two hours, they shared all their hearts. Truth and tears mingled and melded them together. The King watched the couple from afar, smiling. There would be a castle wedding soon. Two were becoming one.

He then looked westward and frowned. Evil never rests.

****

Two weeks later, a lone rider ascended the path up to the gate of the dark fortress. He was quickly ushered in to a shadowed throne room where evil brooded.

"You have news?"

"Is there still a reward for information about the girl?"

Ubel shifted on his throne, grasping the hilt of his sword with his one good, strong arm. A jagged scar ran across his face. The hate was livid in his eyes. "Tell me, and you will receive your reward."

"She lives. And word is, she will soon marry."

He leaned back into his dark throne, evil possessing his soul, ghost pains pulsating his missing hand. "No, she will never belong to someone else," he vowed.

"She will be mine or she will die."

Other Books by the Author

Seven Royal Laws of Courtship
The Teenage Years of Jesus Christ
The Childhood Years of Jesus Christ
The 21 Tenets of Biblical Femininity
The 21 Tenets of Biblical Masculinity
Is Your Youth Group Dead or Alive?
Mountain Lessons
Grace Will Lead Me Home
104 Teen Bible Lessons
Did God Put a Book Inside of You?

Stay in the Castle Series

Stay in the Castle
The Warrior Prince
The Chosen One
The Prodigals

The Teenager's Guide Series

A Teenager's Guide to Character, Success & Happiness
A Teenager's Guide to the Invisible Creation
A Teenager's Guide to Healthy Relationships

Ultimate Goal Publications

Order by phone or online
(812) 665-4375
www.stayinthecastle.com